MINI CLASSICS
THE
MAGIC
CARPET

RETOLD BY STEPHANIE LASLETT
ILLUSTRATED BY CAROLE SHARPE

SHOOTING STAR PRESS

TITLES IN SERIES I AND III OF THE MINI CLASSICS INCLUDE:

SERIES III

© Parragon Book Service Ltd

This edition printed for:
Shooting Star Press, Inc.
230 Fifth Avenue–Suite 1212,
New York, NY 10001

Shooting Star Press books are available at special
discounts for bulk purchases for sales promotions,
premiums, fund-raising, or educational use. Special
editions or book excerpts can also be created to
specification. For details contact: Special Sales
Director, Shooting Star Press, Inc., 230 Fifth Avenue,
Suite 1212, New York, New York 10001.

ISBN 1-56924-251-8

Printed and bound in Great Britain.

There was once a Sultan of the Indies who had three sons and a niece. The eldest Prince was called Houssain, the second Ali, the youngest Ahmed, and the Princess, his niece, was called Nouronnihar. The Princess was the daughter of the Sultan's young brother who had died when she was quite young and so the Sultan had brought her up with his own family. He hoped one day to marry her to a powerful neighbouring prince.

But as she grew older he was alarmed to see that all three of his sons had quite fallen in love with her. They argued constantly about who should ask for her hand in marriage until finally the Sultan called them all before him.

"Since you cannot agree on this matter, I have decided you shall all travel far away, each to a different country. As you know, I love things which are unusual and out of the ordinary and so I promise my niece in marriage to whoever brings back the most extraordinary rarity as a gift to me."

Eagerly the Princes agreed, each thinking himself most likely to find just the thing to please the Sultan. And so, with a sum of money to cover their expenses,

they set out from the gates of the city the next morning. That night they lodged at an inn and the next morning all solemnly agreed to meet there again in exactly one year's time. Then each took a different path in search of treasure.

Prince Houssain, the eldest brother, went straight to the city of Bisnagar, the capital of a neighbouring country. There he found lodgings for himself and after stabling his horse, set off to explore the town's bazaar.

To his great delight he found shops and stalls selling the most wonderful variety of goods: fine porcelain from Japan, silken brocades from Persia and China, beautifully painted puppets from India; and when he came to the goldsmiths and jewellers he was quite dazzled by the light sparkling from the bright diamonds, rubies and emeralds.

Bisnagar was certainly a most impressive city and the air was sweet and fragrant with the scent of roses wherever he went.

11

After visiting almost every shop in the city, the exhausted Prince sat down for a rest outside a merchant's stall. He drank a cup of thick, sweet coffee and contentedly watched the world go by. Soon a pedlar passed by carrying a small brightly coloured carpet.

"Buy my carpet!" he cried. "Just thirty purses of gold!"

"Thirty purses of gold?" thought Prince Hussain to himself, much surprised, for the carpet looked threadbare and well worn.

But when he questioned the pedlar the man replied, "Believe me, even forty purses of gold would be a good price for this is no ordinary carpet. Whoever sits on it will be carried wherever they wish to go."

When the Prince heard this he decided his search was over. The carpet would make a splendid gift for his father, the Sultan, for it was certainly a great rarity. He told the pedlar he would be happy to pay forty purses of gold if he could prove that the carpet did indeed transport its passenger to wherever he wanted to go. The man was happy to oblige and soon they were both sitting cross-legged on top of the carpet in a room behind the merchant's stall.

"Take me back to my lodgings!" cried the Prince and in the twinkling of an eye, there they were, safe and sound. Well, he did not need much persuading after that and handing over the forty purses of gold, he eagerly rolled up the carpet and congratulated himself on his good fortune.

"My brothers will never find anything quite so marvellous as my carpet," he chortled. "The Princess Nouronnihar shall be mine!"

It would be many months before he had to meet his brothers once again, so Prince Houssain passed the time by exploring the country of Bisnagar, meeting the people and learning their customs. The time passed quickly and as the year came to its end Prince Hussain asked the magic carpet to return him to the inn.

In a trice there he was, and there he waited patiently for his brothers.

Meanwhile, the middle brother, Prince Ali, had travelled to Persia and joined a camel caravan which took him to the capital, Schiraz. He lost no time in exploring the city and soon found himself in the bazaar, surrounded by merchandise of every description. Amongst the pedlars who passed back and forth was a man holding a small ivory telescope.

"Thirty purses of gold for this fine telescope!" cried the pedlar.

"He must be mad!" thought Prince Ali. "How can a little telescope be worth that much money?" So when the pedlar next came by he demanded to see the telescope and discover what made it so valuable.

Willingly the pedlar let him look. "This is no ordinary telescope," he explained, "for when you look into it, you can see whatever you wish to see."

Disbelieving, the Prince held
it up to his eye and wished to
see the thing that he held
most dear, his sweet Princess
Nouronnihar. There she was in
the telescope! Nearly dropping
it in his surprise, he watched
as she brushed her long hair.
Prince Ali now felt sure that
this telescope was the most
valuable thing in the world
and quickly he paid the pedlar,
thinking all the while that his
brothers would never find
anything so rare as this.

He passed the following months exploring the country of Persia before meeting up once again with the caravan and returning to the inn, as he had arranged with his brothers. There he met Prince Hussain and together they waited for Prince Ahmed.

Now the Sultan's youngest son had taken the road to Samarkand. Like his brothers, he headed straight for the bazaar and had not been there long before he heard a pedlar calling, "Thirty five purses of

gold for this beautiful apple!"
Prince Ahmed could hardly
believe his ears. Such an
enormous sum of money for a
humble apple? Surely not!

"Show me that apple," he
demanded of the pedlar. "How
can it be worth so much money?"

"From the outside this fruit
looks perfectly ordinary," agreed
the pedlar, "but believe me when
I tell you that this apple is of
enormous value to mankind and
whoever possesses it will be
master of a great treasure."

"This apple will cure sick people of whatever disease or illness ails them. They will recover immediately and have perfect health. All they have to do is sniff the fruit!"

Prince Ahmed was most impressed. "But how can I believe you?" he asked cautiously. The pedlar came closer. "Just ask anyone in Samarkand about this apple and they will all tell you the same thing. Many merchants here have been cured by this self same fruit," and indeed many people approached them and confirmed what the pedlar said. One old merchant laid his hand on the Prince's sleeve.

"Why not come with me and we can test the apple," he said. "I have a friend who is dangerously ill and not expected to live much longer. Let us try the apple on him." And so they went to a nearby house and the experiment was carried out. Sure enough, the apple was proven to be just as effective as the pedlar had promised. The deal was struck, the gold handed over and soon Prince Ahmed was the proud owner of the healing apple.

The months passed and eventually he, too, arrived back at the inn to meet his brothers.

Proudly they showed off their
new possessions, each secretly
thinking their own the best. But
when Prince Ali came to look
through his telescope he was
dismayed to see the Princess
lying close to death upon her
bed. Quickly they sat on the
magic carpet and Prince Houssain
wished them straight to her room.

In a trice the magic carpet
carried them to her side. Prince
Ahmed held his apple under her
nose and they all waited with
baited breath.

31

To their great delight, the roses slowly returned to the Princess's cheeks and she opened her eyes, sat up and asked for her maids to dress her, just as if she had been roused from a sound sleep. The Sultan had been greatly concerned for her health but now he arrived breathless by her side and was told that the three Princes had saved her life and that if it had not been for the swift action of Prince Ahmed, death would surely have awaited her.

Then Princess Nouronnihar thanked the three Princes and welcomed them home. The Sultan embraced each son in turn, well pleased with their part in his neice's miraculous return to good health.

The next day it was time for the Princess to present their rarities and they met in the Great Hall of the palace. Prince Houssain unrolled his magic carpet, Prince Ali proudly handed over his ivory telescope and Prince Ahmed held up his apple.

35

"Come, Father," said Prince Houssain. "You must decide which one of us saved the Princess and so wins her hand!"

The Sultan sat thinking for a long time as the sun slowly sank in the west. How could he make a fair decision when each of his sons had played a part in saving the life of his beloved niece?

At long last he got to his feet. "My sons," he said gravely. "It is impossible for me to make a just decision in this matter. It is true that Prince Ahmed's apple did

cure the Princess — but he would not have known she was ill without Prince Ali's telescope and would have been unable to reach her in time without Prince Hussain's carpet. Each one of you is equally worthy of the Princess." He shook his head. "I must decide this matter by some other means. Go and fetch bows and arrows and meet me on the great plain where the horses are exercised. Whoever shoots their arrow the farthest shall win the hand of Princess Nouronnihar."

So they all met on the great plain
with an excited jostling crowd of
courtiers and ministers. Prince
Houssain shot first and his arrow
travelled a long way. Then Prince
Ali released his arrow and it
overtook his brother's and landed
some distance ahead. Then it was
the turn of Prince Ahmed, but he
shot his arrow so far that it could
not be seen! Everyone believed
that he had shot the farthest but
they would have to find the
arrow to prove this and, try as
they might, it could not be found.

Eventually the Sultan decided
that as the arrow was lost, he
would declare Prince Ali the
winner and so the announcement
was made and preparations began.
Prince Houssain was so grief-
stricken that he would not attend
the wedding feast but left the
court and became a hermit. Nor
did young Prince Ahmed take
much delight in the celebrations
for he was determined to find his
arrow. While the wedding guests
made merry, he hunted the great
plain in search of his arrow.

Further and further he travelled
until at last he reached some
steep and craggy rocks. There to
his astonishment he found his
arrow lying flat upon the
ground. Nearby was a cave and
just inside the entrance Prince
Ahmed found an iron door.
Behind it a steep passage led
him into a magnificent hall and
he scarcely had time to look
about him before he became
aware of a beautiful lady and
her maidservants standing at the
far end of the room.

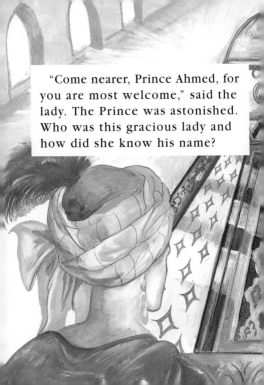

"Come nearer, Prince Ahmed, for you are most welcome," said the lady. The Prince was astonished. Who was this gracious lady and how did she know his name?

"I am the daughter of a powerful genie and Fairy Paribanou is my name," continued the lady. "I saw your bow and arrow contest and felt that you deserved a happier fate than marriage to Princess Nouronnihar. I seized your arrow from the air and carried it to the rocks, where it lay hidden among the crags. Now it lies within your power to make the most of the opportunity which presents itself to you," and with this the Fairy Paribanou looked tenderly at the Prince and blushed.

Then he realised that she was offering herself as his wife and he could hardly believe his good fortune. Why, she was even more beautiful than Nouronnihar! Her voice was warm and kind, her bearing graceful and, as he could see from the grand palace in which he stood, she was blessed with great riches.

With a loudly beating heart he knelt before her. "Madam, if you would consent to let me find true happiness with you, I would be the happiest man alive!"

"I pledge you my love," replied the Fairy, "and now you are my husband and I am your wife." And so it was that the Prince Ahmed found himself married. Then they were fed with excellent meats and wines and exquisite desserts and when their meal was over, his new wife led him through the palace and showed off her diamonds, rubies, emeralds and pearls and each room was filled with greater treasures than the last until the Prince could take no more.

"If you think my palace is so beautiful," laughed the Fairy, "you should see that of my father, the Chief of the Genies. And just wait until you visit my gardens! But we will leave that for another time. Night draws near and it is time for the wedding feast."

And so, by the light of scented candles and as the court musicians played sweet music, they ate dish upon dish of rare delicacies off fine gold plates, while the delighted guests celebrated the marriage of Prince Ahmed

and Fairy Paribanou.

So it was that the pair found great happiness together, but after six months had passed the Prince longed to see his father once again.

"I ask you one thing," said Fairy Paribanou as he prepared to leave. "Do not tell your father of our marriage or where you have been. Just let him know you are happy and leave it at that."

And so the Prince arrived at the Sultan's palace and his father received him joyfully.

He had been sadly grieved by his son's mysterious disappearance.

"Tell me where you have been," he begged. But the Prince remembered the Fairy's request and only replied that he had been safe and well. Then the Sultan reluctantly accepted that this was all he would learn of his son's long absence and made the Prince promise to visit him more often in the future, and the Prince gladly agreed.

Three days later he returned to Fairy Paribanou and time passed happily as before. Over the following months, he remembered his promise to his father and visited often, each time on a fine horse, dressed in grand clothes with many servants in attendance. The Sultan's Grand Vizier watched the Prince with growing suspicion.

"Young Prince Ahmed has grown very rich and powerful," he whispered in the Sultan's ear. "Powerful enough to raise an army of his own and topple you from the throne, perhaps."

The Sultan refused to listen to these rumours but the Grand Vizier was so persistent that at last he decided to spy on his son. He instructed a clever sorceress to follow Prince Ahmed and find out where he was living.

When it was time for the Prince to return home to Fairy Paribanou, the magician hid by the craggy rocks and tried to see exactly where he went, but it seemed to her as if the whole royal company simply vanished from sight. She was quite unable to see the magic gate through which they entered the palace of Fairy Paribanou. Disappointed, she returned to the Sultan and told him the news.

"You must use all your cunning to discover where he goes," urged the Sultan, and so the magician returned once again to the rocks. The next time Prince Ahmed emerged from his secret hideaway the sorceress had a plan. She lay down and, resting her head against a rock, moaned as if in pain. As the Prince rode by he caught sight of her lying helpless and straightaway wheeled his horse around and went to her aid. The artful sorceress raised her eyes to his and in a trembling voice explained that she had been taken ill on her journey.

Quickly he ordered his servants to carry her into the palace. "Have no fear, for help will soon be at hand," he told her reassuringly and the cunning magician sighed gratefully.

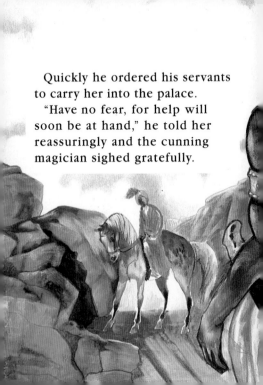

But when the Fairy Paribanou laid eyes on the woman she saw at once through her deceit. Pulling the Prince to one side she said, "This woman is not so ill as she makes out. I believe she means to harm you, but have no fear for I will always protect you."

And so the Prince continued on his journey to visit his father, the Sultan. While he was gone the sorceress was carried to a bed and laid on gold brocade cushions and covered with a fine silver quilt. Then the Fairy's servants brought her a special drink. "This is the Water of the Fountain of Lions and will cure you of all your ills," she was told and sure enough, before an hour had passed, the magician was up and out of bed, pretending to be much recovered. The servants led her to their mistress, the Fairy Paribanou, and when the magician saw her seated on a huge gold throne in the splendid hall she was much amazed by the beauty and grandeur of the Fairy and her secret palace.

Fairy Paribanou knew that the woman was a sorceress and had tricked her way inside but she decided to let her go and see what she would do next.

The magician, with many thanks for the kind hospitality she had received, left the palace and returned straightaway to the Sultan. Quickly she told him all that she had seen; the beautiful Fairy, the great riches Prince Ahmed now owned and the grand palace where they lived. "Indeed, sire," she said. "I believe there is indeed a danger that the Prince is now powerful enough to raise an army and force you from your throne."

The Sultan truly believed that his

son would never do such a thing for he had a good, kind nature, but after further discussion with the distrustful Grand Vizier and his council he was persuaded that the risk was too great to ignore.

"You must have him killed immediately," advised his ministers, but the magician had a better idea. "Ask your son for presents when he comes to visit. He will have to ask his wife, the Fairy, for help and after a while she will become so tired of his demands that she will send him away."

Then the sorceress pondered on what the first present should be.

"When you go into battle you take a great army," she said at last. "Why not ask Prince Ahmed for a new tent as a gift and proof of his love? But this must be a special tent; large enough to shelter your entire army against bad weather, but small enough to carry in the palm of your hand."

The Sultan thought long and hard before asking his son for such a gift for he loved him and did not want to cause trouble for him in

his marriage. And Prince Ahmed
on hearing his father's request
was deeply troubled for he did
not want to offend his wife by
asking her this favour.

At last he confessed to his wife
that he had a request to make.

"Hither to I have been content
with your love and have never
asked you any other favour, but
my father, the Sultan, wishes for
a gift which I cannot give him."
And when Fairy Paribanou heard
his story she was not the least
troubled and called for a servant
to bring her the largest pavilion
in the palace. In walked a girl
holding a rolled up cloth in her
hand. Prince Ahmed was not
impressed.

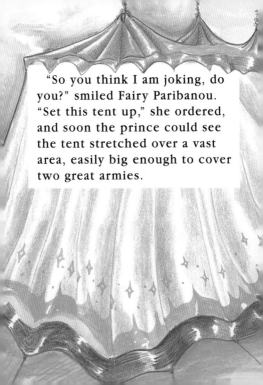

"So you think I am joking, do you?" smiled Fairy Paribanou. "Set this tent up," she ordered, and soon the prince could see the tent stretched over a vast area, easily big enough to cover two great armies.

When the Prince showed it to his father, the Sultan was much impressed and thanked his son heartily, but was not yet satisfied.

"Son," he said, "there is one other thing which I would dearly love to own. I hear that your wife, the Fairy Paribanou, has a spring of the most wonderful water guarded by fierce lions, which cures all kinds of fever and illness. If you care about my good health, please bring me a bottle of that water and prove to me that you are a kind, dutiful son."

But when the Prince returned and hesitantly explained this latest request to the Fairy, she shook her head in worry.

"This request is not so easily met," she replied, "for the spring is guarded by four fierce lions. While two sleep, two remain awake and so there is great danger in fetching the water. But never fear, I will protect you from them." She picked up a ball of thread from the basket at her side. "This will help you find the secret spring. When you leave the gates of my palace roll the ball along the ground in front of you and it will lead you to the Fountain of Lions. You must ride a fast horse and lead another behind you, laden with a sheep cut into four quarters. When the lions see you they will be after your blood, but stay calm. Throw them the sheep and they will soon forget you. Then ride as quickly as you can to the fountain and fill your bottle with water. The lions will be so busy feeding that they shall not notice you go."

The next day Prince Ahmed did
as the Fairy said and, sure enough,
when the lions smelt the sheep
they showed no interest in him
at all. Soon he was riding towards
his father's palace with the water
safely in his bottle.

He strode into his father's hall,
bowed low before him and
presented his new gift. The Sultan
was much impressed and most
curious to know how his son
had been able to get past the lions
and fill his bottle with water. "Who
is protecting you?" he asked.

And so the Prince told him all about his wife, the Fairy Paribanou, and described the magic powers she had shown.

The Sultan pretended to be very glad that his son had married such a wonderful wife, but secretly he was jealous of his success. Bidding his son farewell, he called for the sorceress and asked her advice.

"You must ask one more favour," she said. "Tell him to bring you a man just one and a half feet tall, with a glossy black beard that trails after him upon the ground, and carrying a long iron bar upon his shoulder for a weapon."

Prince Ahmed was much dismayed for he believed that such a man could surely not exist. Sorrowfully he explained his problem to the Fairy Paribanou and to his surprise she laughed aloud. "But there is no difficulty at all with this request," she smiled, "for this little man is my own brother, Schaibar! He may not look like me for he is exactly as your father described, but we do indeed share the same father."

In the centre of the courtyard burned a fire in a beautiful gold brazier. The Fairy sprinkled a special perfume into the flames and soon Prince Ahmed could see a small man walking towards them through the smoke with his staff upon his shoulder.

A long black beard was draped over one arm and his moustache was so long that he had curled it around in loops before tucking it over his ears and out of the way. He wore a grenadier's cap and small, deep-set eyes blazed in his large head. Hunch-backed, he stood before them and scowled fiercely. "Who is this man?" he growled.

"Why, this is my husband, dear brother," replied Fairy Paribanou gently. "This is Prince Ahmed, son of the Sultan of the Indies."

Schaibar bowed low before the Prince. "Your servant, sir," he said gravely. "If I can be of any assistance, you have only to ask." Fairy Paribanou stepped closer to him. "The Prince's father has a burning curiosity to meet you," she said. "Could you accompany him to the Sultan's palace in the morning?" Willingly, the little man agreed and so they retired to have supper together. Then, Fairy Paribanou told her brother of all that happened between the Prince and his father.

Now Schaibar was ready and prepared for any danger.

The next day they arrived at the gates of the Sultan's city but when the people caught sight of this strange little man, so terrifying did they find him that they ran and hid themselves and so the Prince and Schaibar rode through empty streets until they reached the gates of the palace. Here the guards turned heel and fled and so at last, silent and alone, they came to the great hall and there sat the Sultan on his throne.

Boldly Schaibar strode up to the dais and spoke out.

"You have asked to see me," he said in a loud voice. "Well, here I am. What do you want of me?" But the Sultan was so overcome by the sight of this hideous little man that he clapped his hands over his eyes and could not say a word. Outraged by this rude reception, Schaibar lifted his iron bar and brought it down upon the Sultan's head, killing him on the spot.

Prince Ahmed was powerless to

prevent him and before many more minutes had passed, the ferocious little man had worked his way through the Sultan's entire council, lashing out with his quarterstaff and slaying all who stood in his way.

"That does with all the Sultan's so-called advisers. They certainly gave him bad advice!" declared Schaibar, satisfied at last.

One man was left cowering behind the throne and that was the Grand Vizier who had first sewn the Sultan's seeds of doubt.

He had caused much trouble
between the Sultan and his son
but as Schaibar raised his bar
once more, the Prince quickly
stepped in front of him.

"Enough of this terrible
execution," he cried. "Let this
man go free," and so the Grand
Vizier was allowed to get to his
feet. Schaibar glared up at the
cowering Vizier.

"There is one person left I
wish to see," he said. "Send for
the wicked sorceress who
meddled in this affair."

Soon the grovelling woman was brought before them and loudly she begged for mercy, but all in vain, for with one stroke of his bar, fierce Schaimar despatched her, saying, "Now pretend you are ill, you deceitful woman."

Then Schaimar banged his staff upon the ground three times.

"Let it be known throughout the city that from henceforth, Prince Ahmed, my brother-in-law, is proclaimed Sultan of the Indies and unless all citizens immediately acknowledge him as their master, then they, too, will receive the treatment I have given the Council here today."

Quickly the cry went up and spread throughout the streets outside the palace as far as the city walls themselves.

"Long life to Sultan Ahmed! Long may he rule!"

Then Ahmed was clothed in royal robes and sat on the throne to receive the vows of loyalty from his new ministers. Later that day he fetched his wife, the Fairy Paribanou, and with great pomp and grandeur she was declared Sultaness of the Indies.

As for Prince Ali and Princess Nouronnihar, they were given a large province of their own where they lived happily for the rest of their lives.

The new Sultan sent a message to his brother, Prince Hussain, inviting him to choose whichever province he might like for himself, but the Prince replied that he had grown to love the solitude of the land where he now dwelt and asked nothing more than to be left in peace to enjoy it.

The Sultan proved himself a fair ruler and so all ended well for the three sons of the Sultan of the Indies — and the magic carpet? Why, nobody knows what became of that!

The Magic Carpet belongs to one of the greatest story collections of all time: *The Tales of the Arabian Nights*, also known as *The Book of One Thousand and One Nights.* These stories were first heard many hundreds of years ago and include *Ali Baba and the Forty Thieves* and *Sinbad the Sailor*.

They were originally told by the beautiful Princess Scheherezade to the suspicious Prince of Tartary, who had threatened to behead her at daybreak, but her tales were so exciting that, as the sun rose, he longed to hear how they ended and so pardoned her life for one more day, until after one thousand and one nights Scheherezade had won his trust and his heart.